Sophie Spikey

Has a Very Big Problem

in the same series

William Wobbly and the Very Bad Day
A story about when feelings become too big
Sarah Naish and Rosie Jefferies
Illustrated by Amy Farrell
ISBN 978 1 78592 151 3
eISBN 978 1 78450 411 3

Rosie Rudey and the Very Annoying Parent
A story about a prickly child who is scared of getting close
Sarah Naish and Rosie Jefferies
Illustrated by Amy Farrell
ISBN 978 1 78592 150 6
eISBN 978 1 78450 412 0

Charley Chatty and the Wiggly Worry Worm
A story about insecurity and attention-seeking
Sarah Naish and Rosie Jefferies
Illustrated by Amy Farrell
ISBN 978 1 78592 149 0
eISBN 978 1 78450 410 6

Sophie Spikey

Has a Very Big Problem

Sarah Naish and Rosie Jefferies

Illustrated by Amy Farrell

Jessica Kingsley Publishers
London and Philadelphia

First published in 2017
by Jessica Kingsley Publishers
73 Collier Street
London N1 9BE, UK
and
400 Market Street, Suite 400
Philadelphia, PA 19106, USA

www.jkp.com

Library of Congress Cataloging in Publication Data
A CIP catalog record for this book is available from the Library of Congress

British Library Cataloguing in Publication Data
A CIP catalogue record for this book is available from the British Library

ISBN 978 1 78592 141 4
eISBN 978 1 78450 415 1

Printed and bound in China

Introduction

Meet Sophie Spikey and her family

Sophie Spikey lives with her mum, dad, brother William Wobbly, and sisters, Rosie Rudey and Charley Chatty. The children did not have an easy start in life and now live with their new mum and dad. All the stories are true stories. The children are real children who had difficult times, and were left feeling as if they could not trust grown-ups to sort anything out, or look after them properly. Sometimes the children were sad, sometimes very angry. Often they did things which upset other people but they did not understand why.

In this story, Sophie has a very big problem. She worries about asking grown-ups for help and tries to sort everything out herself. Sometimes this means she gets into a bit of a pickle and feels all hot and blotchy. Sophie's mum is good at guessing when Sophie needs help, and is helping Sophie to feel safer about asking. Written by Sophie's mum and her sister (who did not like asking for help), this story will help everyone feel a bit better.

Sophie Spikey did NOT like to ask other people for help.

When she was two, her new mum tried to help her put her coat on. Sophie Spikey said, "ME do it."

Today, Sophie Spikey has a very big problem. She has lost her shoes. Again.

She had looked EVERYWHERE for them, but they had simply disappeared.

Sophie often found that her things just disappeared.

She thought her dad might hide her stuff.

Or maybe her older brother, William, had stolen them just to be nasty.

Sometimes she felt REALLY spikey about that.

Sophie was VERY CROSS that someone had taken her shoes, but she NEEDED them to go to the shops with Mum and her sister.

She liked going to the shops with Mum.

Mum said, "Sophie come on, we're going now!"

She didn't say anything to her mum, because she
did NOT want anyone to know that her shoes were
missing.

Sophie's head felt very busy and hot.

THEN she had a BRILLIANT idea!

She remembered that her mum had put her old shoes in the bin. The bottom of one of the shoes was all loose and Sophie had kept tripping over it.

Sophie took the old shoes out of the bin and quickly pulled off the floppy bottom bit. Once they were on her feet they looked as good as new! Sophie was VERY proud of herself.

Her head stopped feeling hot and busy.

She didn't say anything to her mum. She didn't need to.

She had sorted it out ALL BY HERSELF.

Everything was going very well. Sophie, her mum and sister had been to the supermarket, and now they were off to the more boring outside shops. It started raining.

Sophie's foot kept feeling wet, squishy things. The outdoor pavement was wet and stony.

Suddenly, Mum looked at Sophie and said, "I've noticed that you are walking a bit strangely. Have you hurt your foot?"

Sophie Spikey didn't say anything. She concentrated very hard on the interesting patterns on the pavement. She wondered how many squares there were on the whole pavement.

Sophie knew her mum would make a disappointed face at her if she found out about the new shoes being lost.

Sophie did NOT like grown-ups making disappointed faces at her. It made her feel all hot and blotchy.

The more Mum looked at her, the more she stared at the pavement. The more she stared at the pavement, the more she thought about her shoes.

The more she thought about her shoes, the more her tummy and chest squeezed and whooshed together.

Mum said, "I know something is not quite right, but we can sort this out together."

Sophie knew this was a trick. She looked at the floor so she didn't have to see Mum's disappointed face. Her face felt all hot and blotchy again.

Mum noticed Sophie was wearing her old shoes. There was suddenly a lot of twitchiness in her face. Sophie felt the hotness go all over her body. Mum looked at the bottom of Sophie's shoes.

"Oh dear, your sock is all black and wet. Your foot must be very cold. I think we need to go and have a nice hot drink to warm you up."

The Spikey bit of Sophie wanted to say, "No I'm fine, leave me alone..." but the Sophie part of Sophie wanted a hot chocolate. Very much.

While they were all drinking hot chocolate, Mum said, "I wonder if you couldn't find your new shoes, but didn't want to ask me to help you?"

Sophie concentrated hard on looking at the patterns in her hot chocolate.

Mum said, "When you were very tiny, before you lived with me, you had to sort everything out for yourself. Sometimes, it might feel like there is still only you to sort things out. Don't worry, my job is to help you and we will just keep practising, until one day you will be able to ask me to help you."

Mum bought Sophie some 'emergency plimsolls' to wear home, so her foot stayed dry and warm.

When they got home, Mum helped Sophie to find her new shoes. They had been under her bed the whole time!

Sophie was VERY happy to find her new shoes.
She could still feel the warm hot chocolate feeling
in her tummy too.

That feeling seemed to be lasting a very long time, she thought...

The End

A note for parents and carers, from the authors

This book was written to help you to help your child.

Sophie Spikey has many of the behavioural and emotional issues experienced by children who have suffered developmental trauma, and therefore attachment difficulties. You can see in this book that Sophie does not like to ask for help, is overly independent, and often overwhelmed by feelings of shame. You will have noticed how Sophie finds it difficult to communicate her feelings, and to acknowledge any need for assistance in the illustrations and story.

We provide training to parents, adopters and foster carers, who have said to us that they often feel out of their depth, and do not know what to say or do when faced with these issues. This story not only gives you valuable insight into *why* our children behave this way, but also enables you to read helpful words, through the therapeutic parent (Sophie's adoptive mum), to your own child.

This story not only names feelings for the child, but also gives parents and carers therapeutic parenting strategies within the story. It features some techniques which you can try in your own family:

- **'Naming the need'** – The parent 'names the need' and relates Sophie's overly independent behaviour back to her early life experiences.

- **'Wondering aloud'** – The parent uses 'wondering aloud' to help to identify reasons, without asking 'why'.

- **Touch** – Many of our children function at a much younger emotional age, and never learned to control their emotions (self-regulate) as young babies. When our children are very upset, angry or spiralling out of control, simply placing a calm hand on their shoulder can help them to calm and to self-regulate. This kind of touch is not expected to be reciprocated. 'Mum' touches Sophie within the story, to connect and regulate. She also gives Sophie permission to feel the way she does and reassures her that she will wait while Sophie 'keeps practising'.

Sarah is a therapeutic parent of five adopted siblings, now all adults, former social worker and owner of an 'Outstanding' therapeutic fostering agency. Rosie is her daughter, and checked and amended Sophie's thoughts and expressed feelings to ensure they are as accurate a reflection as possible. Together, we now spend all our time training and helping parents, carers, social workers and other professionals to heal traumatised children.

Please use this story to make connections, explain behaviours and build attachments between your child and yourself.

Therapeutic parenting makes everything possible.

Warmest regards,

Sarah Naish and Rosie Jefferies

If you liked Sophie Spikey, why not meet her siblings, William Wobbly, Rosie Rudey and Charley Chatty

---

William Wobbly and the Very Bad Day

A story about when feelings become too big

William Wobbly is having a very bad day. He didn't want to go to school and when he got there things just got worse. The wobbly feeling got bigger and bigger and BIGGER until...

Something happened to William Wobbly when he was very little, which makes it hard for him to understand or control his feelings. Luckily, his new mum is here to help with his wibbly wobbly feelings.

Written by a mum who understands, and her daughter (who used to have a lot of wobbly feelings), this is a story for children functioning at age 3–10 who struggle with sensory overload.

Rosie Rudey and the Very Annoying Parent

A story about a prickly child who is scared of getting close

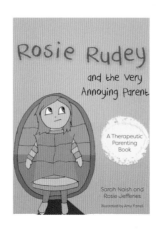

Today Rosie Rudey has had enough!

"Rosie, put your coat on, it's cold outside."

"Rosie, bring your sandwich box to the kitchen, please."

"Rosie, stop being nasty to your brother."

LEAVE ME ALONE, she thinks.

Rosie did not have an easy childhood, which has made her build a hard shell around herself so no one can get in. Luckily, her new mum knows just how to help soften Rosie's hard exterior.

Written by a mum who understands, and her daughter (who was also a bit prickly), this is a story for children functioning at age 3–10.

Charley Chatty and the Wiggly Worry Worm

A story about insecurity and attention-seeking

Charley Chatty likes to talk. Charley talks so much that her mouth gets dry but there's just so much to say!

"Why is the pavement brown?"

"I have got two shoes. Everyone has two shoes."

"I can hear the radio. Who is on the radio? Why is there a button on the radio?"

Sometimes, Charley's imagination takes over and she tells stories about things that didn't really happen. She doesn't mean to but she likes how it makes her feel important and the wiggly worry worm inside her belly goes away.

Written by a mum who understands, and her daughter (who also liked to tell tales), this is a story for children functioning at age 3-10.